THE STORY OF FUZZYPEG THE HEDGEHOG

The Story of Fuzzypeg the Hedgehog
first published in Great Britain in 1932 by William
Heinemann Limited

This edition first published in Great Britain in 1984 by

Octopus Books Limited
59 Grosvenor Street
London W1

© Text Trustees of Alison Uttley
Literary Property Trust 1984

This arrangement © 1984 Octopus Books Limited

Second impression, reprinted 1985

ISBN 0 7064 2205 8

Produced by
Mandarin Publishers Limited
22a Westlands Road
Quarry Bay, Hong Kong

Printed in Hong Kong

THE STORY OF FUZZYPEG THE HEDGEHOG

BY ALISON UTTLEY
ILLUSTRATIONS BY MARGARET TEMPEST

OCTOPUS BOOKS LIMITED

Early one summer morning, when the white mist lay over the fields like a soft blanket, old Hedgehog uncurled himself and rolled out of bed with a flop! on the floor.

'Don't wake Fuzzypeg,' called Mrs Hedgehog, warningly, as he rubbed his bruised shin, and struggled with a sheet which was all mixed up with his prickles, 'and don't tear the bedclothes.'

Hedgehog managed to get unravelled without spoiling the leaf-linen sheet of which Mrs Hedgehog was so proud. He stooped over little Fuzzypeg, who lay curled up in his bed, a small dusky ball of prickles.

'He'll be a grand fellow when he is grown up,' said he to his wife.

Over the head of the bed hung a string of

coloured bobbins, a present from Little Grey Rabbit, who lived in the house on the edge of the Wood, and on the floor lay a poppy-head drum.

Hedgehog went downstairs with his prickles lowered, lest they should brush the whitewash off the ceiling, and walked into the kitchen. Mrs Hedgehog polished him up with a duster, and gave him a clean brown handkerchief.

He opened the door and took down a small wooden yoke, which hung on a low branch of a sycamore tree.

He slung it across his shoulders with the two chains hanging, one on each side. On the hooks of these he hung two little wooden pails, and, hitching them up, he started off to get the milk.

Don't be late,' called Mrs Hedgehog, as she shut the door. 'Remember, breakfast is at six o'clock today. It is Fuzzypeg's birthday.'

The mist was so thick he could scarcely see, but he trotted down the beaten path, through the furze gate, as prickly as himself, into the fields. The grass was ready for cutting, and Hedgehog was up to the ears in red sorrel and buttercups. Soon he was soaking wet with the heavy grass pushing against his knees.

He walked straight through the meadow, under a five-barred gate, which gave little room for his yoke and pails, to another field of short pasture grass. A low deep sound of breathing reached him, and out of the whiteness appeared a herd of cows, dozing as they stood waiting for the sunrise.

oo-up, Coo-up,' called Hedgehog, and a roan-and-white Cow raised her head and watched him unhook his pails and remove the yoke. Hedgehog gave her a nudge; 'Lie down,' he commanded, and she obediently lay down.

'There's going to be a fine sunrise this morning,' said the Cow.

'How do you know that?' said Hedgehog, as he squatted down beside the Cow, and drew the tinkling stream of milk into the little pail.

'By the clouds, like curds and whey,' answered the Cow. 'When they are like butter, it will be dull,' she continued.

'And what happens when the clouds are like eggs?' asked Hedgehog, smacking his lips at the word 'eggs.'

'Then it will rain!' said the Cow, decidedly.

'Talking of eggs, I shouldn't mind one myself,' Hedgehog remarked.

'Plenty in the hen-house,' replied the Cow.

Hedgehog was silent for a few minutes, as he milked steadily, his mind running on eggs. The little pails were soon frothing over with milk, so he politely thanked the Cow, and took up his yoke.

Off he walked, slowly now, with brimming pails, across the meadows to the house where lived Grey Rabbit and her friends, Hare and Squirrel.

Hedgehog knocked at the door, and Grey Rabbit, in her white collar and cuffs, fresh as a daisy, opened it.

'You are early this morning, Hedgehog,' she said.

'Yes, Grey Rabbit, it is my little Fuzzy-peg's birthday,' replied the Hedgehog.

ow old is he?' asked Grey Rabbit, at once excited and interested.

'A year—half-grown up,' said the Hedgehog.

'Wait a minute, and I will send him a present,' said Grey Rabbit, and she scampered upstairs to the attic, whilst Hedgehog measured out the milk.

She came running down with a hen's egg.

'It's a Boiled Egg,' she said. 'I boiled it all day. Little Fuzzypeg can play ball with it.'

Hedgehog thanked her, and picked a cabbage leaf from the garden. He made it into a bag, and put the egg inside. Then he tied it to the milk pail.

'Where's that Boiled Egg?' he heard the voice of Hare crying. 'Grey Rabbit, I want that Boiled Egg for my breakfast.'

So he hurried away before the Hare could take it back.

He walked down the garden path, along the lane, and across a big field to Mole's house. Moldy Warp lived underground, in a large castle, with many passages and rooms. The Hedgehog went to one of the back doors and knocked three times.

The door opened a crack, and a little pink hand stuck out, holding a stone milk-jug.

'You are early this morning, Hedgehog,' said the Mole. 'I was in my larder arranging things on the shelves. On one I put Bluebottles, Blue-bells, Blue-berries; on another Red Currants, Red Herrings, Red Radishes; on another Green Cabbage, Green Chutney, Green Grasshoppers; on another Black Berries. . . .'

'I'm afraid I must go,' interrupted the

Hedgehog. 'It is little Fuzzypeg's birthday today.'

'Wait a minute and I will send him a present,' said the Mole. He disappeared down the passage, and Hedgehog measured out the milk.

When he returned he carried a hen's egg.

'It's a Scrambled Egg,' said he. 'I had to scramble under a hay-stack and scramble back with it.'

'Oh, thank you, kind Moldy Warp,' said the Hedgehog, putting the scrambled egg with the boiled one in his cabbage-leaf bag. 'Fuzzypeg *will* be pleased; he always wanted a scrambled egg.'

He walked across the field, through a gap, and under a stone wall, to an old black house.

He knocked at the door and a Rat answered. Hedgehog felt slightly nervous at Rat's house, and never turned his back, although Rat seemed a friendly fellow.

'Here's the milk,' said Hedgehog, quickly.

'You're in a hurry today,' said the Rat.

'Yes, it's my little Fuzzypeg's birthday.'

'And how old is he?' asked the Rat.

'A year,' said Hedgehog, feeling uneasy.

'I will send him a present,' said the Rat, who wanted to be on good terms with Hedgehog.

He ran to his cupboard and took out from among clubs, blunderbusses, traps and springs, an egg. 'It's a Poached Egg,' he said solemnly. 'I poached it last night from the hen-house.'

Hedgehog put it in his cabbage bag with the other eggs.

'Thank you, Rat,' he said politely, as he

14

walked backwards out of the yard and through the gate to the field.

There was one more house to visit, and that was Red Squirrel's, a house in the Pine tree. Hedgehog knocked at the door, and Red Squirrel, who was always full of jokes, came tumbling downstairs and bumped into Hedgehog, nearly upsetting the rest of the milk.

'You are early with the milk, Hedgehog,' said he, throwing his jug into the air and catching it.

'Yes,' said the sober Hedgehog, who did not like such pranks. 'It is little Fuzzypeg's birthday and I must be quick. He is a year old today.'

'Your little Fuzzypeg's birthday? I must send him a present,' and he ran indoors, and pattered up and up the long stairs, to the top of the tree.

H e came down carrying an egg, a dark-brown egg.

'It's an Old-Laid Egg,' said he, 'the same age as Fuzzypeg,' and he laughed as he gave it to Hedgehog.

So Hedgehog put the Old-Laid Egg with the others and hurried home with the remainder of the milk.

'How kind everyone is!' he thought, as he trotted rapidly across a ditch, and through gaps and gates to his house under the sycamore tree.

Fuzzypeg was sitting on a little chair, waiting for his bread and milk, and Mrs Hedgehog was making the toast when Hedgehog arrived.

'All these presents for Fuzzypeg,' said he, putting the eggs on the table, and he told them the story of each one.

Fuzzypeg had the Scrambled Egg for breakfast, and divided the Poached Egg between father and mother. The Old-Laid Egg and the Boiled Egg he kept for toys.

After breakfast, while Mrs. Hedgehog washed the little wooden pails and tidied up, Hedgehog went out with his son to play 'Rolling.' They climbed up a hill with the eggs, curled themselves into balls, and rolled down to the bottom.

'Bumpitty Bump!' went Fuzzypeg.

'Bumpitty Bump!' went old Hedgehog.

'Bumpitty Bump!' went the Boiled Egg.

S quishitty Squash!' went the Old-Laid Egg.

Such a smell arose! All the little earwigs, caterpillars, woodcreepers, beetles, flies, and grass-hoppers, who were walking about on the hill, taking the morning air, fainted, and Hedgehog and Fuzzypeg took to their heels and ran all the way home. After a time they ventured back to get the Boiled Egg, and Hedgehog vowed he would punish the bad Red Squirrel, by giving him no milk. But Fuzzypeg said: 'It was rather funny, you know, to see everyone stretched out. I should like an egg like that for a Weasel.'

When evening came and the sun went down in a sea of gold, Hedgehog gave Fuzzypeg his present—a green parcel.

Fuzzypeg opened it with trembling paws.

Inside the wrapper was a little white cage, made of the pith of rushes, curiously woven, like a basket, with a handle. Two small black creatures lay within.

As he held the cage, twilight came, and the stars began to peep in the green sky. The little creatures sent out a beautiful soft light, so that the cage was like a fairy lantern.

'What are they?' asked Fuzzypeg, whispering in happy wonder.

'Glow-worms,' replied Hedgehog. 'Two tame glow-worms. Feed them and treat them kindly, and then you can let them loose in the hedge-garden.'

Fuzzypeg hung up the cage from a hook in the ceiling, and the room was filled with the delicate light.

But when he came down the next day, the

glow-worms were fast asleep, and so they remained till evening, when they shone like captive stars.

Hedgehog was very fond of eggs, and began to poach. He hunted in barns and outhouses, in hedges and woodstacks, but usually he found nothing, for Rat had been there first.

Then, on a lovely September day, he had a great adventure. He was strolling through the fields, near the farm, holding Fuzzypeg's hand, and keeping a sharp look-out for stray eggs, when suddenly the hens began to cry and hiss and scream.

'Help! Help! Help! Save us! Run for your life!' they cried, and they rushed with wings outstretched and legs wide apart to the shelter of the farm.

All except a Speckledy Hen, who was too frightened to move. She stood staring at an adder, which glided nearer and nearer.

Fuzzypeg trembled and stayed very still, but Hedgehog sprang at the adder's tail, and held it with teeth and hands. The adder whipped round and darted its tongue at Hedgehog. Fuzzypeg screamed and shut his eyes, but, equally quickly, old Hedgehog had curled himself like a furze ball, a solid mass of spears, with the end of the snake's tail inside.

Over and over again the adder tried to bite Hedgehog, only to be met by the sharp, dense prickles. Old Hedgehog never let go until the adder lay dead.

The Speckledy Hen came up, quivering and shaking.

'Hedgehog, you saved my life,' said she.

'It's nothing. Pray don't mention it,' said Hedgehog, modestly. A crowd from the farmyard hurried across to congratulate him.

'Three cheers for Hedgehog!' cried the barn-door Cock. 'Cock-a-doodle-*Doo!* Cock-a-doodle-*Doo!* Cock-a-doodle-*Doo!*'

'It's months since I tasted Hadder Pie,' said Hedgehog. 'My wife will be glad of this,' and he slung the adder across his back, and went home with the admiring Fuzzypeg.

After a fine dinner of Adder Pie, Fuzzypeg ran out to play 'Hide and Seek' in the larch wood, with his cousins, Tim and Bill Hedgehog, who lived in a cottage in the wood.

I say, you fellows!' said he, thrusting out his quills, and holding his nose in the air, 'I say! My father killed a Nadder! He pounced on it! Yes, *pounced* on it, and held the tip-tippit of its tail till it was dead.'

'That's nothing,' said Bill Hedgehog, scornfully. 'My father pounced on a Lion's tail and held it till it was dead!'

Fuzzypeg ran in and out of the slender trees, treading on the larch needles, hiding among the ferns, pretending to enjoy himself, but his heart was heavy and his quills drooped. He did not even stop to talk to a young rabbit, who peeped longingly from her door, wishing to be invited to join in the game.

'I don't want to play today,' he said at last, and he walked home through the bracken, expecting to meet a full-grown Lion, and wondering what he should do.

His mother was sewing a pair of leather shoes for him, with a gorse needle, and his father sat at the door mending a milk pail.

'Mother,' said he, 'if my father met a Lion, could he pounce on its tail and hold tight till it was dead?'

'Of course he could,' replied Mrs Hedgehog, looking up from her sewing, and old Hedgehog proudly rattled the milk pail, and wisely said nothing.

'He could fight an elephant, I expect,' said Fuzzypeg to himself, and he held up his head again.

'Tell me the tale of how Grey Rabbit killed the Weasel,' he implored his mother, and she told him the old story.

He made up his mind to be very brave like his father and Grey Rabbit.

very morning the grateful Speck-ledy Hen laid an egg under the Sycamore tree, and every day Mrs Hedgehog divided it neatly into three parts, for Hedgehog, Fuzzypeg and herself. She wanted to repay the kindness of the Hen, so one day she made a hay-seed cake.

'Take this to the Speckledy Hen,' she said to Fuzzypeg. 'Do not dawdle on the way home. Walk on the little green path under the hedge-row, not on the broad white road across the fields. There are dangers about,—Weasels, Stoats, Snakes, and worse.'

'What shall I do if I meet a Danger?' asked Fuzzypeg.

'Roll up in a ball, and keep your face hidden.'

'Suppose I meet a Lion?'

is mother laughed and gave him a gingerbread to eat on the way. 'You won't meet a Lion,' said she.

He trotted through the fields, picking a few mushrooms and blackberries. He sniffed at the honeysuckle, far above his head, and admired the red rose-hips. When he got to the Low Meadow he met the Speckledy Hen.

'Mother sent you a hay-seed cake,' said he, 'and she thanks you for the nice eggs.'

'How deliciously sweet it smells!' said the Hen, taking the brown cake. 'Now come with me and I will show you where the finest acorns fall.'

She took him up to a great old oak tree, and he picked the young fallen acorns. Then she led him to a ditch to watch the frogs play 'Leap-frog.'

By the time he started home it was getting late.

The blackbirds were calling, 'Hurry up, hurry up,' to their children, and the thrush was practising her music for next day's wood-concert.

'You are late, little Hedgehog,' called a Robin, as he flew on his way with a letter in his beak.

'Stop and play a minute,' said the Hare, who sat warming his ears in the slanting rays of the setting sun.

Fuzzypeg stopped a minute, and a minute, and a minute, whilst the Hare tried to explain noughts and crosses to him.

Then he turned again for home, singing and shouting for joy in the evening.

''Ware Stoat! 'ware Stoat!' cawed a Rook, flying to his family, and the excited cry of the Blackbird in the hedge decided him.

H e would go along the white path and leave the hedge-row.

He hurried along the broad easy road, thinking of his supper, and the game of noughts and crosses he would teach his father. Suddenly he saw a great, white, curly-haired animal bounding towards him, leaping in the air like a lamb.

He hesitated, and the animal saw him. It roared, and sprang towards him with frightful springs.

'A Lion,' thought poor Fuzzypeg, dropping his acorns and mushrooms. He gathered himself bravely together, and prepared to spring on its tail, but the animal had no tail, or if it had, it was as short as Grey Rabbit's.

'A Lion without a tail!' cried Fuzzypeg, and he curled himself up in a ball and kicked off his shoes.

The Lion bounced into him, and got a bunch of prickles in his nose. 'Bow-Wow! Bow-Wow! Ough! Ugh!' he cried, retreating.

Fuzzypeg peeped out between his prickles, and saw the Lion advancing again to the attack. He put his head under his arm and waited.

'Bow-Wow! Bow-Wow! Ow! Ow!! Ow!!!' roared the Lion, with more prickles sticking into him, and he turned and ran to—Oh! Horrors! Fuzzypeg saw a great Elephant advancing, also without a tail!

'Good Dog, Spot; keep off him!' cried a voice, and Fuzzypeg was picked up, put in a large handkerchief, and carried away.

He had just made a hole, and was preparing to escape, when he was dropped with a thump.

ook what Spot and I found, Daddy! A young Hedgehog!'

'Put it in the garden, Tommy; it will catch slugs.'

'No, I won't, I *won't* catch slugs!' squeaked Fuzzypeg. 'Let me go home. My father is a great Hedgehog, and he once killed a Lion.'

Tommy took no notice, but carried the Hedgehog to the garden, and put him on the path. Slowly Fuzzypeg uncurled and had a peep. Then he bolted for the gate, but he was not quick enough, for Tommy seized him, and put him under an enormous flower-pot. He brought him a bowl of bread and milk, and left him for the night.

When no little Hedgehog came home, old Hedgehog went out to look for him, along the green lanes and byways.

He traced him to the field where he had met the Hare, and on the ground there he found a little paper with O's and X's. Hedgehog could not read it, so he put it in his pocket, and followed the track along the white path. A bundle of acorns tied up in a tiny dirty handkerchief lay there, some mushrooms screwed up in a dock-leaf, and a pair of red shoes.

As he examined these, he felt a pair of eyes staring at him, and, turning, he saw the Stoat in the hedge.

Old Hedgehog never knew how he got home to his wife. He was in despair as he showed her the shoes and the pathetic little bundles. But Mrs Hedgehog would not give in.

'You must go this very night to Grey Rabbit's House to ask if they know anything,' she said. So Hedgehog set off again, under the golden September moon.

H e knocked at the door, and Squirrel answered.

'No, we don't want any milk tonight, thank you,' said she, shutting the door.

'Please, ma'am, it's my little Fuzzypeg, he's lost.'

'Does anyone know where Fuzzypeg Hedgehog is?' she called into the house.

Grey Rabbit came running with a half-knitted sock in her paws, and Hare came with a little green book he was reading.

'I've seen him,' said Hare. 'We met in the Low Meadow, and we had a little game of noughts and crosses. He will be quite good at it when he grows up, if he practises.'

Hedgehog took the paper from his pocket.

'Yes, that's it, the very paper,' said Hare.

hat happened then?' asked Hedgehog.

'He just ran on and on, and I ran the other way.'

Grey Rabbit then spoke. 'I am so sorry, Hedgehog. I advise you to see Wise Owl.'

'Wise Owl? Oh no, not Wise Owl!' cried Hedgehog.

'Why not?'

'Because,' and here Hedgehog hesitated, embarrassed, 'because he might be hungry, you see.'

'If you wave a white handkerchief for a truce, you will be safe,' said Squirrel, quickly, as if she did it every day.

'Can you lend me one, or even two?' asked Hedgehog. 'We only use brown ones at our house.'

Little Grey Rabbit tied two white handkerchiefs to his prickles, and he went into the great Wood.

Wise Owl was out hunting when Hedgehog rang the silvery bell, which hung on the door of the old oak tree. So he sat down to wait, feeling very small and lonely. High up among the pointed leaves he could see the kindly Moon, which had run with him through the Wood, and away, caught among the fountain leaves of a silver birch, was a cluster of twinkly little stars, 'like a Hedgehog in the sky,' he thought. He crept closer to the tree and held his nose against the rough warm bark. It was comforting.

'Too Whit, Too Whoo,' came nearer and nearer, and Wise Owl, who had heard the bell far away, flew to his house, carrying something which Hedgehog preferred not to see.

'Who are you?' he asked the little creature down below.

lease, Sir, I'm Hedgehog the Milkman.'

'What do you want?'

'Please, Sir, I've lost my little Hedgehog, and Grey Rabbit thought you could find him for me.'

The Owl was flattered and shook his feathers.

'Perhaps I can,' he replied proudly, 'but I must be paid.'

'Anything you like,' said the Hedgehog.

'Well,' said Wise Owl, considering, as he stroked his beak, 'I will have a quill for a pen and a can of milk, and a new-laid egg. Bring them tomorrow at dawn, and you shall have news of your son.'

Hedgehog thanked him and went home, keeping a wary eye for Stoats, Weasels, and Badgers on the way.

Wise Owl flew with wide sweeping wings over the fields that night looking for little Hedgehog, but nowhere could he see him.

'Stoat, have you seen little Hedgehog?' he asked a shifty-eyed light-haired fellow, creeping along the hedges with a club in his hand.

'No, Sir,' said Stoat. 'I only saw Milkman Hedgehog a moment.'

'If you see him, report to me,' said Wise Owl, sternly.

'Yes, Sir,' said Stoat, touching his slouched hat, and grinning a crooked grin. 'I wish I had seen him,' he muttered when Wise Owl had flown away.

'Rat, have you seen little Hedgehog?' the Owl asked a dark poacher, creeping under a wall with a twisty wire in his hand.

o, Sir. I sent him an egg for his birthday, but I've not seen him.'

'Report to me if you do,' said Wise Owl.

'Yes, Sir,' said the Rat, touching his cap, and hurrying on.

'Yard-dog, have you seen little Hedgehog?' the Owl asked a curly white dog, sitting outside his kennel, singing to the moon.

'Yes,' answered the dog, 'I've seen him, but I shall tell you nothing about him. I belong to the House, and you belong to the Wood,' and the dog proudly shook his chain and continued his song.

'He must be somewhere near,' thought the Owl, so he searched the lawn and pig-sty, the drying-ground and orchard.

A little sound caught his keen ears, as he

flew slowly over the garden, a sound of weeping and soft sobbing.

'Mother, Mother, Grey Rabbit, Father, Moldy Warp. Come! Come! Oh! I'm so lonely and lost!'

The sounds came from a large inverted flower-pot, standing firmly in the rhubarb bed. The Owl flew down and looked through the hole in the top.

The sobbing ceased, for little Fuzzypeg was terribly alarmed to see a bright eye instead of the far cluster of stars.

'Is that you, little Hedgehog?' asked the Owl.

'Yes, it's me,' said the little creature, trembling.

'Help is coming,' said the Owl, and he flew away home, for his work was over.

At dawn came the Hedgehog through the great Wood, carrying a can of milk, a goose-quill for a pen, and a new-laid egg. He rang the bell and waved the handkerchiefs. Owl, who was just getting ready for bed, looked through the door.

'Put them down there, Hedgehog. Your son is safe under a flower-pot in the farmer's garden.'

Hedgehog thanked him and started home at a run, calling on his way for Little Grey Rabbit, Hare, Squirrel, and Moldy Warp. Mrs Hedgehog ran to the door when she heard the patter of little feet, and she joined them. They all ran through the fields, Hare and Little Grey Rabbit leading, Squirrel coming next...

H edgehog and Mrs Hedgehog panting after . . .

. . . and Moldy Warp far behind.

They squeezed under the gate (except the fat Hare, who had to climb the wall), and ran across the lettuces and carrots, down the little path between the gooseberry bushes, to the red rhubarb, where stood an enormous plant-pot.

'Are you there, Fuzzypeg?' called old Hedgehog.

'Yes, Father, are you?' answered a small faint voice.

'Yes, we are all here,' said Hedgehog; 'Squirrel, Hare and Grey Rabbit, and Moldy Warp is on the way.'

He turned to the animals. 'All push, and over the plant-pot must go.'

So they pushed and they pushed, but the

plant-pot didn't move, and they pushed and they shoved, and the plant-pot *still* did not move.

'Steady, boys! Now! All together! SHOVE!!' called Hedgehog, but still the plant-pot did not move.

A large Rat strolled up. 'What are you people doing?' said he.

'Little Hedgehog is under this plant-pot,' explained Hedgehog, raising his prickles.

'Oh, he's found, is he? Wise Owl asked me to keep a look-out for him. But you will never move that thing if Hare pushes one way and you all push the other.'

Hare blushed and went over to Grey Rabbit.

'Now, heave ho!!!' shouted Rat, but as they all pushed away from him, the plant-pot still did not move.

hey stuck their little feet in the ground, and puffed and panted and bumped their shoulders, and got pricked by Hedgehog, and kicked by Hare, and frightened by Rat. Little Hedgehog inside shouted, 'Push harder! Push harder!'

They rested a moment, and wiped their hot brows with the two handkerchiefs on Hedgehog's prickles.

Then Moldy Warp turned up.

'Not that way,' said he, quietly. 'If the pot fell over, you would all be squashed. This is the way.'

He planted his feet firmly, and with nose and hands dug rapidly into the soil by the flower-pot. Earth flew in a shower, and in a few seconds he disappeared down the tunnel

he had made. The animals waited, breath-
less.

Then a tiny snout appeared, and little
Hedgehog crawled up the tunnel, to be
hugged, prickles and all, by old Hedgehog
and his wife. A minute later came Mole,
wiping his lips.

'I stopped to finish his bread and milk,' he
explained. 'It was a pity to waste it.'

He rammed the soil down in the tunnel,
and the happy procession started home.

'Don't forget to tell Wise Owl that I found
little Hedgehog,' called the Rat as he ran off.

'Come into the garden and have some
refreshments,' said Mrs Hedgehog, when
they got back. So they all sat under the
sycamore tree, whilst she spread a cloth on
the grass.

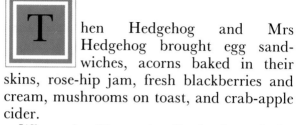

Then Hedgehog and Mrs Hedgehog brought egg sandwiches, acorns baked in their skins, rose-hip jam, fresh blackberries and cream, mushrooms on toast, and crab-apple cider.

When the Hare, the Squirrel, and the Little Grey Rabbit went home, they each took a small quill pen, which the grateful Hedgehog had made for them; but Moldy Warp wouldn't have anything, for, he said, digging was more in his line than writing, and he had everything he wanted in his castle under the Ten-Acre field.